J. P. Miller

Rourke
Educational Media

A Division of
Carson
Dellosa
Education

Before Reading: *Building Background Knowledge and Vocabulary*

Building background knowledge can help children process new information and build upon what they already know. Before reading a book, it is important to tap into what children already know about the topic. This will help them develop their vocabulary and increase their reading comprehension.

Questions and Activities to Build Background Knowledge:

1. Look at the front cover of the book and read the title. What do you think this book will be about?
2. What do you already know about this topic?
3. Take a book walk and skim the pages. Look at the table of contents, photographs, captions, and bold words. Did these text features give you any information or predictions about what you will read in this book?

Vocabulary: *Vocabulary Is Key to Reading Comprehension*

Use the following directions to prompt a conversation about each word.

- Read the vocabulary words.
- What comes to mind when you see each word?
- What do you think each word means?

Vocabulary Words:

- construct
- documents
- patrol
- recruit
- supervisors
- trades

During Reading: *Reading for Meaning and Understanding*

To achieve deep comprehension of a book, children are encouraged to use close reading strategies. During reading, it is important to have children stop and make connections. These connections result in deeper analysis and understanding of a book.

 Close Reading a Text

During reading, have children stop and talk about the following:

- Any confusing parts
- Any unknown words
- Text-to-text, text-to-self, text-to-world connections
- The main idea in each chapter or heading

Encourage children to use context clues to determine the meaning of any unknown words. These strategies will help children learn to analyze the text more thoroughly as they read.

When you are finished reading this book, turn to the next-to-last page for **After-Reading Questions** and an **Activity**.

TABLE OF CONTENTS

THE RIGHT FIT

When you think about important jobs in the military, you might think of people planning missions or commanding troops. However, some of the most important jobs in the military are the **trades**. These jobs help keep people safe, make missions successful, and more.

The US Military has several branches: the Army, Air Force, Navy, Marines, and Coast Guard. All of them have jobs for tradespeople.

trades (traydes): particular jobs or crafts, especially those that require working with the hands or with machines

Have you ever taken an important test? If you want to join the US Military and work in a trade, you might take one of the most important ones of your life. Some people take a test called the Armed Services Vocational Aptitude Battery (ASVAB) in high school. This important test lasts 2.5 hours. It will decide what job a **recruit** might have in the military.

When a **recruit** enters the US Military, they go to Basic Military Training. After that, some of the recruits who are going into the trades attend trade school. Others get on-the-job-training at their first military base.

recruit (ri-KROOT): someone who has recently joined the armed forces or any group or organization

A QUICK START

No college or experience? No problem! Many military programs offer recruits job training for beginners. Military members also have opportunities to attend college with assistance from the government.

SPECIAL SKILLS

It's the day of the annual fitness test that determines if military members are fit for duty. The test is possible because Administrative Assistants organized it. They contact all of the people needed to give and take the test. Later, they record the military members' scores and send them to **supervisors**.

Administrative Assistants do many important jobs. They keep official **documents** organized. They run offices. They plan events and gather information. They also keep records of how military members are paid.

documents (DAHK-yuh-muhnts): pieces of paper containing official information
supervisors (SOO-pur-vye-zurs): people who watch over and direct the work of other people

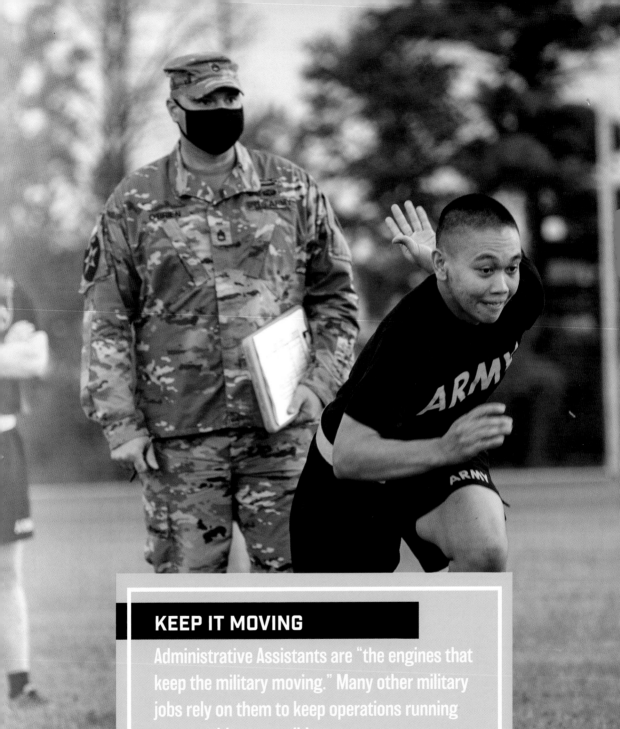

KEEP IT MOVING

Administrative Assistants are "the engines that keep the military moving." Many other military jobs rely on them to keep operations running as smoothly as possible.

To do well as an Administrative Assistant, you should be organized. You must be able to plan well and work well with others. Good reading and writing skills are also important.

How do you make a city in a desert? Civil Engineers know how. They make the plans to bring in materials and build a temporary military site. They **construct** buildings, build runways, and set up fencing. They check the work to make sure that it is safe. Finally, they arrange repairs if they are needed. Before long, rows of sand-colored tents are lined up beside each other. The tents house dining, recreation, and military members.

Civil Engineers are responsible for constructing and repairing military buildings. Some handle dangerous jobs such as clearing fields full of explosive material. They also help during emergencies by planning cleanup efforts.

construct (kuhn-STRUHKT): to make or build something

If you want to be a Civil Engineer, it is important to like and be good with math. You must be organized. Civil Engineers sometimes check on sites around the world, so you should also like to travel and be outside.

TO THE RESCUE

Civil Engineers were an important part of the rapid response following the attack on the World Trade Centers. They provided heavy equipment, helped move rubble, and helped with rescue efforts.

Waves splash high and land is nowhere in sight as the Boatswain Mates work. They have checked the boat for safety before heading out to sea. They are searching for and rescuing people who are lost at sea.

Search and rescue missions are just one of their tasks. Boatswain Mates also take care of the ship, help train others, and stand watch for security. They are trained in firefighting in case a fire breaks out on the ship.

SAFETY ON THE WAVES

The United States Coast Guard (USCG) handles protection, search and rescue, and law enforcement in the water for the US Military. The Department of Homeland Security runs it in times of peace. However, during war time, the Navy might run it instead.

To do well as a Boatswain Mate, it is important to be able to solve problems. You must be able to do your job in dangerous situations. You should also have good physical fitness and enjoy being around water.

"Never bring a problem to your officer; only bring solutions."

— Corey Scott, Petty Officer Second Class, US Coast Guard

Like most cities and towns, the US Military has Law Enforcement Officers. Their responsibility is to make sure that laws are followed and enforced. They also are responsible for protecting military members and property from enemies.

Law Enforcement Officers have many of the same powers and duties as those in local communities. They can pull a suspect over, do searches, and arrest people. They carry weapons and **patrol** areas to look for criminals.

patrol (puh-TROHL): to walk or travel around an area to watch or protect it or the people within it

If you want a career in Law Enforcement, it is important to want to help your community. You should have good physical fitness. You should also be okay with going into dangerous situations.

PAWS FOR LAWS

Military dogs are very important to Military Law Enforcement. They are used to track drugs, explosives, and hidden threats. Military dogs work for ten years before they can retire.

Getting military members and supplies from place to place is an important job. It takes a lot of planning and teamwork. Transportation Specialists use airplanes, boats, railways, trucks, and even gigantic ships to get the job done.

Transportation Specialists manage vehicles as well as what goes on them. They conduct driver training and issue government driver's licenses to military and civilian employees. They schedule safety checks and help decide when to buy new vehicles.

"If you're not early, you're late!"
— Steven Albano, Sergeant First Class, United States Army Reserve (Retired)

USMC 522870
E0846

SHIP

Good Transportation Specialists are very organized. They are good at planning. If they don't move the supplies and equipment where they are needed, no one can do their job, so Transportation Specialists must be reliable.

ON THE ROAD

The US Interstate System is a highway system 47,856 miles (77,016 kilometers) long that connects 48 states. It was built to help move military members and supplies faster and more directly from base to base.

A LIFETIME CAREER

Tradespeople in the US Military organize and manage important equipment such as boats and trucks. They use their special skills to protect and even rescue military members. For many people, the trade they learn in the US Military turns into a lifetime career.

Do you like learning and solving problems? Are you good at organizing and communicating? If so, you could be a great Tradesperson!

MEMORY GAME

Look at the pictures. What do you remember
reading on the pages where each image appeared?

INDEX

AFTER-READING QUESTIONS

1. Where do military recruits get job training?

2. Why is it important for Administrative Assistants to be organized?

3. How long do military dogs work before they can retire?

4. Why was the US Interstate System built?

5. What do Boatswain Mates do?

ACTIVITY

Act like a Transportation Specialist and plan a trip for yourself and a group of friends. Think about all of the things that you would need to get everyone from one place to another. Draw a map of your trip and make a list of all the supplies you will need.

ABOUT THE AUTHOR

J. P. is a veteran of the United States Air Force living in Metro Atlanta, Georgia. She now writes children's books that augment a child's classroom experience. J. P. is very excited to combine her love for writing with her military experience to produce the Careers in the US Military series.

© 2021 Rourke Educational Media

www.rourkeeducationalmedia.com

Quote sources: Steven Albano, interview with author. Corey Scott, interview with author.

PHOTO CREDITS: cover: ©PO2 Richard Brahm/U.S. Coast Guard/Department of Defense; page 4-5: ©Cpl. Rachel K. Young-Porter/U.S. Marine Corps; page 5 (top): ©Senior Airman Mya M. Crosby/U.S. Air Force/DoD; page 5 (bottom): ©PO3 Andrew Langholf/DoD; page 6-7: ©Pornpak Khunatorn/Getty Images; page 7: ©antoniodiaz/Shutterstock.com; page 8-9: ©Staff Sgt. Kenneth D. Burkhart/U.S. Army Reserve/DoD; page 10-11: ©SDI Productions/Getty Images; page 10: ©Seaman Apprentice Patrick Dionne/U.S. Navy/Released/DoD; page 12-13: ©Steven Tucker/Us Army/ZUMA Press/Newscom; page 14-15: ©vm/Getty Images; page 15 (top): ©Staff Sgt. Veronica McNabb/DoD; page 15 (bottom): ©US Navy/Sipa USA/Newscom; page 16-17: ©PO3 Aidan Cooney/Coast Guard/DoD; page 18-19: ©Ivan Cholakov/Shutterstock.com; page 20-21: ©Lance Cpl. Mackenzie Binion/U.S. Marine Corps/DoD; page 22-23: ©chris wanders/Shutterstock.com; page 23 (top): ©Sgt. Christopher Bonebrake/DoD; page 23 (bottom): ©A1C Mariam K. Springs/U.S. Air Force/DoD; page 24-25: ©U.S. Navy Grady T. Fontana/Released/DoD; page 26-27: ©Patrik Slezak/Shutterstock.com; page 28-29: ©Senior Airman Mya M. Crosby/U.S. Air Force/DoD

Edited by: Tracie Santos
Cover and interior design by: Alison Tracey

Library of Congress PCN Data

Tradespeople / J. P. Miller
(Careers in the US Military)
ISBN 978-1-73164-352-0 (hard cover)(alk. paper)
ISBN 978-1-73164-316-2 (soft cover)
ISBN 978-1-73164-384-1 (e-Book)
ISBN 978-1-73164-416-9 (ePub)
Library of Congress Control Number: 2020945610

Rourke Educational Media
Printed in the United States of America
01-3502011937